Care Bears™

Wish Bear's Promise

Written by Sonia Sander
Illustrated by Jay Johnson

ISBN 0-439-74414-8

· 12 11 10 9 8 7 6 5 4 3 2 1   5 6 7 8 9/0
Printed in the U.S.A.   First printing, October 2005

SCHOLASTIC INC.

New York   Toronto   London   Auckland   Sydney
Mexico City   New Delhi   Hong Kong   Buenos Aires

Twinkers is Wish Bear's
best friend.
He grants all of her wishes.
"I wish we had lots of
popcorn to eat!"
Wish Bear wished.

"Should you be using
your wishes for popcorn?"
asked Cheer Bear.

"Oh no, Twinkers!" cried Wish Bear.
"I meant popcorn for the
three of us, not all of Care-a-lot."

Wish Bear often shared
Twinkers' wishing powers.

"I wish Share Bear gets
lots of rainbow sap,"
said Wish Bear.

Share Bear got lots of sap.

There was too much!

Next, Wish Bear helped
Grumpy Bear's rocket fly.

It zipped and zoomed
across the sky.
And so did Grumpy Bear!

When Friend Bear's garden
needed a little water, Wish Bear
asked Twinkers to help.

Twinkers helped
Friend Bear to a flood!

Soon, Wish Bear's friends
asked her to stop making
wishes for them.

So Wish Bear wished for
friends who liked wishes.

Twinkers brought her Too-Loud Bear,
Me Bear, and Messy Bear.

Too-Loud Bear, Me Bear,
and Messy Bear loved wishes.

They wanted to make wishes
all the time, even for a
bigger house. Poor Twinkers
was getting tired.

Finally, Wish Bear had to tell her
new friends, "No more wishes."
But then she made a mistake!

Even though she didn't mean to,
Wish Bear wished Twinkers
would be *their* wishing star instead.

"We will give Twinkers back
soon," said Too-Loud Bear.

"But first we need to make a
few more teeny-weeny wishes,"
added Messy Bear.

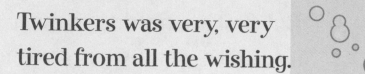

Twinkers was very, very
tired from all the wishing.

He was even starting
to lose his glow.

After one-too-many
clean-up wishes, Twinkers
wasn't glowing at all.

Wish Bear knew what
she had to do.

Wish Bear took Twinkers
to Big Wish. She was the
source of all wishing power.
Big Wish fixed Twinkers!

"I'm sorry," Wish Bear said.
"I forgot that friends should
watch out for one another."

Wish Bear promised
to never forget again.

Big Wish made Twinkers
as good as new.

Wish Bear never forgot
her promise.